jE HARGREAV Adam
Little Mi
Hargrea

D0979190

LITTLE MISS FABULOUS

originated by Roger Hargreaves

TO:

_____

FROM:

_____

EAN

ISBN 978-0-451-53411-8

9 780451 534118

5 0 4 9 9 >

LITTLE MISS
FABULOUS

originated by Roger Hargreaves

Written and illustrated by Adam Hargreaves

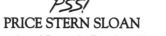

PSS!
PRICE STERN SLOAN
An Imprint of Penguin Random House

Little Miss Fabulous had fabulous hair.

It was long and luxurious and silky, and it shone in the sun like gold.

Every day she liked to try out a different style.

And everybody else thought her hair was fabulous.

So fabulous that they all wanted to copy her.

When she piled her hair up high, everyone else piled theirs up high.

When she wore her hair straight, so did everyone else.

And even when she dyed her hair pink, everyone had to have pink hair as well.

Whatever Little Miss Fabulous did had to be fabulous. After all, she was fabulous.

The only person who did not copy her was Little Miss Splendid.

Little Miss Splendid was jealous of all the attention that Little Miss Fabulous's hair brought her.

She was so jealous that she started a rumor that Little Miss Fabulous's hair was not real and that she wore a wig.

A rumor that Little Miss Trouble decided to put to the test!

To keep her hair as fabulously fabulous as possible, Little Miss Fabulous went to her hairdresser each week.

The most famous hairdresser in town.

Ms. Topknot.

Ms. Topknot is a genius with hair.

There is nothing she can't do.

She even managed to tame Mr. Clumsy's hair!

Now, last week, Ms. Topknot was ill, and she asked Little Miss Splendid to step in for her.

Little Miss Splendid was happy to help out.

At least, she was happy until Little Miss Fabulous came in for her weekly appointment.

But then Little Miss Splendid had an idea.

A rather spiteful and not-at-all-nice idea.

Little Miss Splendid set to work.

In a great flurry of combs and curlers, she
washed and combed and brushed and teased
and blow-dried Little Miss Fabulous's hair.

And when she had finished, Little Miss Fabulous's hair was a big curly, frizzy bird's nest of a ball sitting on her head.

Little Miss Splendid smiled a mischievous smile as Little Miss Fabulous left the salon.

"She doesn't look so fabulous now, does she?" Little Miss Splendid said to herself.

A little later that day, Little Miss Star came into the salon.

"Have you seen Little Miss Fabulous's hair?" exclaimed Little Miss Star.

"I have," said Little Miss Splendid, smiling a sly smile.

"Isn't it amazing?" cried Little Miss Star.

Little Miss Splendid could not believe her ears.

"Quick, you have to give me exactly the same style!" insisted Little Miss Star.

And so Little Miss Splendid did.

And she had to do the same for Little Miss Sunshine and Little Miss Giggles and Little Miss Helpful.

There was a steady stream of people wanting Little Miss Fabulous's hairstyle all day long!

At the end of the day, Little Miss Splendid met Little Miss Fabulous on her way home.

"Why, your hair looks fabulous," said Little Miss Fabulous.

And why do you think Little Miss Splendid's hair looked fabulous?

That's right!

In the end, she had felt she had no choice but to create the same hairstyle for herself.

Well, as they say, if you can't beat them, join them!

MR. MEN   LITTLE MISS

by Roger Hargreaves

SIL-5018

MR. MEN™ LITTLE MISS™
Copyright ©2016 THOIP (a Sanrio® company).
All rights reserved.
Used Under License.

PSS!
PRICE STERN SLOAN

Little Miss Fabulous™ © 2016 THOIP (a Sanrio® company). All rights reserved.
First published in the United States by Price Stern Sloan, an imprint of Penguin Random House LLC.
PSS! is a registered trademark of Penguin Random House LLC. Manufactured in China.

www.mrmen.com

ISBN 978-0-451-53411-8

10 9 8 7 6 5 4 3 2 1

Little Miss
Bossy

 Little Miss
Naughty

 Little Miss
Neat

 Little Miss
Sunshine

 Little Miss
Tiny

 Little Miss
Trouble

 Little Miss
Giggles

 Little Miss
Helpful

 Little Miss
Magic

 Little Miss
Shy

 Little Miss
Splendid

Little Miss
Twins

Little Miss
Chatterbox

Little Miss
Ditzy

Little Miss
Late

Little Miss
Lucky

 Little Miss
Scatterbrain

 Little Miss
Star

 Little Miss
Busy

 Little Miss
Quick

 Little Miss
Wise

 Little Miss
Tidy

 Little Miss
Greedy

 Little Miss
Fickle

Little Miss
Brainy

Little Miss
Stubborn

Little Miss
Curious

Little Miss
Fun

Little Miss
Contrary

 Little Miss
Somersault

 Little Miss
Scary

Little Miss
Bad

Little Miss
Whoops

Little Miss
Princess

Little Miss
Hug

 Little Miss
Fabulous

$4.99 US
($6.99 CAN)

 PSS!
PRICE STERN SLOAN
www.penguin.com/youngreaders
www.mrmen.com

ISBN 978-0-451-53411-8

EAN

9 780451 534118

50499 >